SHIP'S PASSING
[SELECTED WORKS]

also by d.a. peters

Under the Sink [selected works]

SHIP'S PASSING
[SELECTED WORKS]

D.A. PETERS

LULU BOOKS

Raleigh, N.C.

2011

For M.G.—gone but not forgotten.

The world is like a ride in an amusement park, and when you choose to go on it you think it's real because that's how powerful our minds are. The ride goes up and down, around and around, it has thrills and chills, and it's very brightly colored, and it's very loud, and it's fun—for a while.

Many people have been on the ride a long time, and they begin to wonder, "Hey, is this real—or is this just a ride?" And other people have remembered, and they come back to us and say, "Hey, don't worry; don't be afraid, ever, because this is just a ride."

And we kill those people.

"Shut him up! I've got a lot invested in this ride, shut him up! Look at my furrows of worry, look at my big bank account, and my family. This has to be real."

It's just a ride.

-BILL HICKS, Revelations (1993)

Contents

Introduction 15

Ship's Passing. 19

Bad Faith 29

Standing Room. 43

Upper Division 55

Killing the Messenger 69

A Human Condition 83

Curious Branding. 99

Acknowledgements 111

About the Author 113

d.a. peters

Introduction

I didn't think I'd write another collection of stories but here you and I are—not literally, of course. If I am, wave hello.

In December 2010, I lost someone very close to me. I had planned to attend the University of Washington with her: she as a graduate student and I as a commited undergraduate. I didn't find out she killed herself till a month after-the-fact.

As Vonnegut said, "so, it goes. . ."

I stopped writing. I stopped socializing—though I went out for coffee with a dear friend, K.L., a few times. I didn't know where to begin. I didn't want to. Aside from school, I stayed in my apartment: growing a beard and taking care of my sister and my niece. That's all I felt inclined to do. However, the world's larger than I imagined when I finally peered outside the narcissism of my head.

I had to. I saw the alternative.

All I knew was that I needed to get right: I was accepted to a few schools but settled on The Evergreen State College. I knew no one there and hoped no one would bother me.

That just goes to show what an ass I am.

My peers had the decency to bother me with humor and kindness. I was told, frankly, that "panties" reminded A.D. of crime show coroners, that S.S., A.A., and I should create games like the ones I grew up with and that sometimes it's best to laugh when faced with no other alternatives.

So, this collection is, in some ways, an author getting on his feet again. It's me writing after the clouds left. The nights aren't as strange nor as long anymore.

I won't hope that you enjoy the following stories: feel how *you* feel—and have the courage to say as much. The worst that could happen is that your feelings might mean nothing to someone but:

Who wants to be stopped by nothing?

D.A. Peters

October 2011

Introduction

d.a. peters

Ship's Passing

Walt and Ernesto lived in the nursing home for three years before the latter died. They'd met in Rockville. Ernesto fathered a daughter from his first marriage. Walt was his second—marriage that is. They cared for a greyhound. Once, they rode the Metro together—neither of them able to drive—and married in the District on a warm, autumn day not soon forgotten. Ernesto developed Alzheimer's that fall.

So, I'm packing his things. Walt can't do it. He says this as he cleans his glasses with a handkerchief. They're rimless, leaving his blue eyes open.

Putting them on, he says, "I'm older than anyone I know."

I run tape on a new box's spine. "That's impressive."

"Used to be," he says. "Ernesto laughed at that."

Walt stares at the single depression in the bed from where he slept and the lack of a matching one beside it. Ernesto used to wear pastel guayaberas—French cuffed ones. I fold each. For his eighty years, his whole life fits into two U-Haul boxes and a sea-bag. Walt rests his hands on his cane. His eyes trace the outline of the room: taking in the empty easel, the hangers in the closet and the solitary depression in the bed.

"Wish I'd never married the jackass," Walt says.

I disassemble the easel by the window and rub the grease from my palm onto my nursing scrubs. Each hinge folds in on itself. They fall into place—small enough to wrap my hands around. Walt's lips tremble. He takes the glasses off with his thumb and index finger, wiping tears with the back of his hand.

"Leave it," he says.

"You don't paint."

"Leave it."

★★★

No one ever told me this but sex on a beach is a logistical nightmare.

All the sand sticking to sweat-lathered bodies and us ignoring the dry chaffing and rising tide because we really want to orgasm and couldn't wait. It's still fall.

So, January and I are on Assateague's beaches—covered in sand. She says that she's into palm-reading and starcharts now. She wants to go to Tibet or Thailand. "Someplace really spiritual" is how she puts it. "Someplace where the drinks are cheap." She goes to ask if she looked all right—that she felt ill. "Am I okay?"

I ask how her mother is doing and she says that she goes in for dialysis next week. She lights a cigarette. She says, "I wish I could do more" as I stroke the scar above where her left kidney used to be.

"How was work?" she asks. She tilts her head to one side water dripping out of her ear.

I tell her about Ernesto and Walt.

"Jesus," she says. She asks if the other residents ever gave Walt and Ernesto flak—if anyone comforted or could begin to comfort Walt, when Ernesto died.

"Everyone gets it. Finding someone at that age is hard enough."

She's been reading some Buddhist texts and really wants to share them with me—or anyone really. How life and the self are one big dream. How life is disappointment. She stops and adds "don't read into it—you did well, buster." She says it makes sense—that there's got to be more than people decomposing.

"There's a color and a shape," she says. She sits up,

holding the cigarette in her lap and bringing her knees a little closer. She looks at her toes, all ten of them. Wriggling them, she tries to shake the sand loose.

"You won't wind up like her," I say. The words spill out—like sugar in a bowl. They're sweet and soft—they're saccharine and flaccid.

"I could use a drink," she says.

We finish and watch the crabs and barnacles covering nearby rocks. They'd eat us if we sat more still.

***

Julian cheats at cards. He tells the newer residents that his left eye is glass. He has heterochromia. The left looks like a cat's and changes color on occasion—not quite blue nor quite gold. Julian used to work the floors in Vegas during the fifties—tracking the tables for counters.

Walt, Julian, Flo and I sit and play cards. I've already charted for the evening and the LPN doesn't mind if I play till the end of my shift. Cards are best when winter approaches.

"Are you getting any?" Julian asks Flo. He trades in an Ace of Spades.

"Wouldn't you like to know?" She winks. Flo's as big a flirt as him. Their relationship is the worst kept secret in the retirement home. They kiss.

Walt groans and throws his head back.

"I'll call it," he says. Walt lays his cards on the table: a royal flush. "I'm done for the night."

★★★

January and I met underwater. She and I took a marine biology seminar from UCSD. We met at SeaWorld. January welded at an artist commune in La Jolla. She made bookmarkers from steel. The markers took fluid shapes: Celtic knots, ship's wheels and snakes that eat themselves. I asked if I could see one and her eyes lit like roman candles. She showed me the snake writhing, the world wrapped in his scales, and his tail in his mouth. Everything slid into place—like opera gloves.

That night, we French kissed next to the ramp-way leading to the Giesel. The first few months were like that—kissing and groping in the dark and picking each other's clothes off the floor the next morning. We ate Thai food and watched Woody Allen movies. She hugged me one day, the bump in her belly growing, saying she'd sold her work to a gallery downtown. "All of it. I can get a car," she said. We agreed on either Malcolm or Lisa.

Nine months later, long after Malcolm was born and then died on our kitchen floor, we moved to D.C., closer to her family. I followed in a moving van.

★★★

Walt fires a wrist-rocket at passing cars.

"I did this as a kid," he says. "Back in Colorado."

He looks out over the National Cathedral with its Christmas lights up and a half dozen embassies in tow. He holds his fingers out like a gun and aims at the flags. I'm not sure what Belgium did to him.

"You're not allowed to have that, Walter."

"Goddamnit—don't scold me."

"Mr. Ship, I can't let you do that. They'll call the cops."

He takes a breath and sets down the wrist rocket. Grabbing his cane, he gestures toward the chair beside him. I move the day's paper—obituaries open—and sit.

"In Pueblo, my folks had a small house..."

He talks of going down to US Highway 85—of impressing the neighbor kids, mostly boys, while his parents shopped in town. They'd sit on hill—trying to hit the shinier cars. The people who couldn't be bothered to stop. His parents were the generation that left the farms during the Great Depression. So, he'd sit on the hill and mark the brightest car he could see. He'd had his eye on a boy his age, Tom, but all Tom ever did was talk about Suzie. By high school, Walt was alone and Suzie was through with all the Toms, Harry, and Dick in Pueblo. They married and things were quiet until she died. It wasn't until he met Ernesto that he had someone to shoot rocks at cars with.

Walt finishes his story and he's heaving. The phlegm's backed up. I lean him over the railing and pat him on the back as he coughs up the green, mercurial bal. He spits it over the balcony.

I rub my hand on his back and he starts laughing—crying really. I look over to see what he sees. There's a black Mercedes with government plates. The phlegm rests on the sunroof. He looks up and laughs, his blood-shot eyes stamped red in approval.

"I hope it was a politician."

★★★

The note on the fridge door says, "I'm leaving." January drew the snake eating itself.

I take the note down and dial her number while the snows fall. I hold up the picture of the snake against the window pane and wait for the call to go through.

The phone rings—but it rings inside the house. She must've left it. I walk around, looking for it, and it's then that I see January's silhouette against the wall. She sways side-to-side. While we were dating she'd listen to music in her headphones. Maybe I can sneak up, cheer her—like the days when she was sober and I was there more. There's no sound coming from her stereo.

When I open the door, I see why.

★★★

I drive January to the Emergency Room—try to explain that she'd left a note. I keep holding up the picture of the snake eating itself—showing the doctors, explaining to the police what happened. A nurse pats me on the shoulder. "Why can't I go see her?" I ask.

All I can think of is why we bought the high tensile-strength climbing ropes from REI. The officer grimaces at the rope burns on my hand, which shake. The nurse gives me a coffee. The police say I'm free to go.

A doctor tells me that, "It looks like post-partum." He says I should sleep and that they'd keep her overnight. I sit holding her hand—remembering her asking if she was all right on the beach that fall. I blink and my eyes open to dawn.

January comes to and runs her fingers through my hair. She asks to go to the psych ward and says I shouldn't blame myself.

"I just need some time," she says. "You can't fix everything."

★★★

I don't talk to anyone at work. I don't even bother with a leave of absence.

Walter sits outside. He bundles himself in thick coats and what must be a sable hat which dwarfs the man from Pueblo. I sit down next to him and cry. He turns to me and coughs into his handkerchief. His eyes are red and he smells of mouthwash.

I take the wrist rocket from my nursing scrubs and tap it against his shoulder. I wipe tears away with my back hand. He forces a grin. The green rings at the base of his teeth show. He fires a few rocks then passes the wrist rocket back to me.

"Shiniest car?" I ask.

"Shiniest car." I let go of the band and the rock clears the street, then the yard and it strikes the National Cathedral. Glass breaks and lights turn on.

We wait for the next car—as the snakes wrap around in the snow.

d.a. peters

Bad Faith

A lamb fights another lamb on the edge of a ravine. The smaller of the two rears at the larger, black headed one. With a child's cry, the larger one hops backwards, hind legs flailing. His feet search for footing but the lamb falls into the ravine at sunset.

The sun sets. What if I got it all wrong? Maybe the night's rising?

My feet rest on a milk crate. Inside, my girlfriend, Tzi, is putting her son to bed. The Arizona sun sets out near Jerome and a clear yellow ribbon bundles the horizon. I-17 murmurs by, like an inebriate in the back of a bar. Glinted howls of coyotes drive quarry before them. There's an engine block lifted on empty telephone spools next to the doghouse made from mortar, beer cans and cinderblocks. I look at my shirt; grease stains from the night shift at Denny's cover it like an old world map in a Hemingway novel—broken but recognizable shapes.

The screen door opens. Tzi frowns.

"Wouldn't believe what they've been teaching him," she says. She lights a cigarette. "Told him evolution was some hunch—some theory, the way you and I might say 'I got a theory.' God giving babies HIV on account of—and I quote-'Intelligent design.'"

She flicks embers free.

"Next they'll teach her there ought to be something to astrology… you listening, babe?"

I turn toward her, "Always."

"You ain't said a thing all night." She takes a drag from her cigarette.

I can see the woman who grimaced and winked at me as her oldest, then two, threw a cup of cheerios at the congregation's Bishop. The only woman in the Relief Society who called carrots on green jello "a bullshit Mormon affectation." Back when I called her Sister Agnes. Not Tziporrah. Not Mrs. Anežková.

I turn back to the sounds of the lamb in the gully, just past the rise.

"Tzi, you remember when…"

Her cigarette sits in an ashtray—finished. She's inside.

Bad Faith

★★★

I used to be a Mormon missionary. We'd wake at 5:30 every morning, say prayers and study the bible together. The sun would rise, just above the plateaus to the east. You could hear javelinas outside snorting and running circles, startled by a jack rabbit tripping over his own ears. You'd think they'd be extinct.

By 8:00, the pair of us would take our bicycles out and start the descent into town. All the hills remind me of little hobbits borrows, whole families tucked into the horizon, tucked just behind the next hill. From a distance, this place looks uninhabited, even at night given the no streetlight ordinance.

"Got a plan, Elder Watts?" My companion peddled alongside me on the wide, desert-highway shoulders.

"You pack your shorts and a shirt, Kagan?"

He nodded, his helmet sliding off. To this day, Elder Kagan's head is two sizes too small.

"Let's find a use for them. If not, I figured we'd tract out near Bashas'."

When we knock on all the doors in a neighborhood, it's called tracting. Yes, there's a word for kids in black suits waking you up on a Saturday Morning. When we are with members of the local congregation, it's called splits instead. When my companion and I did either, I called boredom.

I made note that that Sunday, we'd teach the eight year olds. A Sister by the name of Anežková invited us. Jesus meek, Jesus mild. She says we'd offer a fresh perspective as missionaries of the Lord. What would you have said?

Me? I remember hearing a comedian, Dave Foley, refer to Jesus as a "failed carpenter."

People laugh when I tell them I used to preach.

★★★

Tzi looks up in the moonlight as I crawl into bed. Her healing heart of a face smiles in a dozen pieces. She runs her fingers along my side, looking at the scar beneath my ribs. I reach for her hand but she presses her breath into my neck. Her black hair nuzzles along my ear.

"I've got work, Tzi."

Her fingers unbutton my shirt and she nibbles on my ear. I feel adrift, like a child making peace with the waves to the west.

"Babe, I work in the morning."

Tzi pulls away with a stare uncertain of all things but anger. She rolls onto her side, tucking her knees to her chest. She pulls the blanket up over her shoulders.

"Everyone has work in the morning."

★★★

Elder Kagan and I met Sweet Jane watering petunias on her front porch. Her granddaughter sent a card requesting us to visit.

"You look like you need some too," she says. Sweet Jane turns off the hose and asks us to sit on her porch.

Preaching is easier to the converted. There's less to buy into, to explain. No need to contextualize ramblings of young boys in New York or the stories families told each other on the way to Jerusalem.

Handing us each a glass of water, Sweet Jane told us a story: her once burned down a catalog advertising Lili St. Cyr—in the middle of her daughter's bedroom. Both of them prayed a lot—and for each other. Neither of them really had their prayers answered.

Sweet Jane hadn't been—nor ever would be—religious. She denounced God as soon as she put the keys in the ignition at 17.

"Good riddance," she said.

Jane'd never married. A jack Mormon—an Easter Catholic, if you will—courted her. The two had a daughter in Washington, D.C. The local church congregation said they'd lived together for decades. "Sin" is what they call it. Happiness is how I saw it and that'd be the tragedy: if two people could just be happy.

He'd cared for her, even proposed but she'd rejected

the notion.

It was then that she came to regret not marrying him. He'd died of an hemorrhagic stroke and left everything to her: meaning the lint in his pockets. She'd put his ashes in the petunias, calling it "poetic that he would not be raised from the dead but he'd at least help the flowers grow."

I remember teaching her about the Mormon beliefs: "No coffee, no sex before marriage, no alcohol."

"Don't tell me what to do, boys. Red meat can be done in excess, right? So could the fat on the edge of the steak.

"I don't want God in my bedroom or over my ta-ble—unless he plans on doin' some eatin'."

We kept telling her that God asks us to give up things as a principle of faith, that we must trust and surrender ourselves to god.

"Did God tell you this? In person?"

"No."

"Why coffee? Why sex? Why not underwater basket weaving?

"Your God's an ass."

She'd smoke her cigarette. Jane's a nihilist sometimes. She takes one look at Elder Kagan and I before smiling.

"Cheer up: there are ends to life sure as the ones

on a jump rope. Love nothing, hate nothing: understand everything."

Sweet Jane looked out over her flowers. Ashes to ashes. Her petunias were still growing when I left Arizona that summer.

★★★

"Can you watch Derrick until the school bus comes?" Tzi gestures over to her oldest. "Just an hour. He can sit in a booth, right?"

I defer to her.

Tzi crouches, looking her boy in the eye.

"Derrick, listen to me. Don't do anything crr-razy. Got that?"

The boy sighs, as if another ten years older. I know the look: I used it whenever my mother reminded me not run scissors even when I wasn't even holding any.

"You got that, Derrick?"

"Yes, Mom."

"Hey, attitude. Watch that at school—your teachers don't love you as much as I do."

Tzi turns toward me and looks through her sunglass.

"Make sure he gets there, okay?" Tzi walks over and kisses me on the cheek. She leans in and whispers, "He looks up to you, you know?"

She kisses me again and hops into her jeep. The horn

honks twice and she's off. Dust kicks up.

Derrick sits on the curb. He reads a comic book.

"You want some hashbrowns, man?" I ask.

He nods his head.

"I'll give you mine."

★★★

My companion and I didn't look so great: we spent as little time as possible in suits. I'd pretend we were charitable but have you ever worn a suit in 100 degree weather? We'd volunteer: helping people clean their property, repair their toolsheds, and for a few weekends helped roll tar paper on the roof of a weathered, string of a man: Jean Baptiste. He kept bees—said that he appreciated the help but that the only thing he liked about Mormons was their bee-like status.

"Workers," he said. "Hard workers."

Jean continued on about bees being a good analogy for Communism: despite the Queen's name, all bees served each other and relied on one another. He says this, slapping the staple gun down: three, two, one.

"They fill each other's needs."

Jean placed down the staple gun and dragged his plate over. The quesadillas didn't need a microwave on that roof. "Any larva can become a queen, a worker, or a soldier—depending on their diet."

"Bees can be anyone, you know?" Jean smiled at this. His jeans were nearly worn through when I nailed the last board down to support our weight.

★★★

"Derrick make it to school?" Tzi asks, stepping out of her jeep. Thick mud runs along the wheel wells.

I wipe my hands on my shirt.

"Yeah. He made it. You cut your hair?"

She grabs her bag from the passenger seat.

"You don't like it, do you?"

"No, babe, I like it—I like it, okay?"

She looks up through the rims of her sunglasses.

"You cut it yourself?" I ask.

"With shears," she says, shaking the dust from the soles of her shoes.

★★★

A middle-aged rancher and his daughter once asked Elder Kagan and me to bless their herds. The sheep sat in a field, freshly shorn, already blessed once by the local medicine man. I know that's not the title. The Navajo medicine man lives a trailer beyond the property line. He's not allowed on one-acre parcel of Yavapai lands, something about his daughter calling off a wedding. So, to spite the tribe, he blessed sheep.

The rancher looked up at us, thick gaps in his gums.

Camp Verde's water has too much arsenic for half the year. He holds the first of his flock up, while Elder Kagan and I squeeze a few drops of olive oil on its head.

I mumbled something about "Heavenly Father." I remember wanting to test that good shepherd title. Maybe not good but at least half-way serviceable, when God isn't drowning worlds for not listening. The news that morning talked about a woman who drowned her baby in the bathtub for not saying grace, for not listening. Thoughts like this made me wonder if I should've blessed the sheep at all.

So, whatever and amen. I tried hard to be earnest, one hand over the other. The consecrated oil starts to get in the sheep's eyes. Elder Kagan choked up. He tried to hold back his laughter. He bit his tongue as he pretended his eyes were closed. Jesus doesn't do his miracles when your eyes are open.

I felt bad at the time. These dibeh were this father's and daughter's livelihood but they're desperate enough to ask two nineteen year-old boys to ask Jesus to impart some of the veterinary training he picked up when he wasn't being crucified.

★★★

The cries return again that evening: the black lamb in the ravine.

"Should we check on it?"

"Might as well," Tzi says.

Tzipporah tosses my .22 over her shoulder, her black crops of hair brushing beneath the sling. Her son marches alongside in the tall grass.

"Derrick, you should go back to the house."

Tzi looks at me and then down to Derrick. "You know the lamb's been down there a day, right?"

Derrick nods his head at Tzi.

Coming on the ravine, we can see the lab: cakes of dirt in its wool, pelvis crushed by a boulder. There's a small pool of blood but the lamb still breathes. Tzi pulls the rifle high into her shoulder.

Derrick tugs at her shorts.

"Mom, he's still alive."

Tzi lowers the rifle.

"Derrick, the lamb's trapped."

Tzi raise the rifle again, eyes resting on the lamb's. Her cheek rests on the buttstock and she exhales.

There's a pop like a kernel of corn. A bit of smoke from the small divot where the bullet entered the base of the neck. The lamb's cries stop.

Derrick looks up at his mother.

"Why'd he have to die, Mom?"

"Baby, he wasn't going to make it. You wouldn't want

to be trapped like he was would you?"

Derrick considers it, rolling his little head side-to-side.

"I wouldn't want to, Mom.

"Can I watch a movie tonight?"

Tzi nods at her son. He sprints ahead to the house, laughing.

We reach the fence, past the engine block.

Leaning against the fence, I think of Tzi's haircut, the dust shaking from her feet and the lamb in the ravine. I spin around, excited and sure, hitting my shin against the empty spool.

"You want to talk, Tzi?"

Tzi continues walking, rifle slung over her shoulder. I reach for her hand. She turns and strokes her chin, hand still gripping the sling.

"I've got work in the morning, Hyrum."

Bad Faith

d.a. peters

Standing Room

Claudia rests her head on her shoulder and stares at the train full of people without pants. Her coffee burns her lips before she stops staring. Not a single person wears pants in this sea of graying boxer-briefs and bikini bottoms and skin.

"Padriac?" Claudia says. She squints at the young man who's moved back in the train.

He turns, unlatching an earphone. His eyes open wider than the Potomac.

"Claudia? My god—I haven't seen you in forever! How—how the fuck are you?"

"I'm pretty well," Claudia says. "You're naked?"

Padriac looks down at his sanguine boxers, black hairs running down his legs. His arms fall open at his sides.

"Oh – that! Haven't you heard?"

"Heard that indecent exposure laws changed?"

"No, no. It's the No Pants Metro Ride. It's this annual improv thing."

"I definitely see that," Claudia says, averting her eyes. "And you wonder why they nearly revoked your student visa."

"Oh—come on. It's for a good cause: you'll make someone laugh—or give a shit less." Padriac lets go of the handlebar and gestures to the other passengers.

"Now?!"

Padriac nods his head, the way a dog would follow a stick.

"Believe me—no one cares and that's the best part!"

Claudia unbuttons her jeans and slides them off, a caterpillar scar running up her thigh. Her black sweater and underwear remain.

"See? No one cares," Padriac says.

★★★

The CCTV cameras mounted at each intersection watch the people below. In 24-hour loops, everyone darts like threads weaving through a loom. If these cameras hold the exposure long enough, the needlework won't show. Thousands of threads pass through the camera's field of vision, most dark with the wearing of winter.

The threads double-back on themselves too in an orderly cross-stitch. To work and from work. To bars and from bars. Even the night crochets its own image, as fluorescent lights flicker to life. The picture grows green. There is no audio feed but it is not without its own music.

Aside from a few homeless men, cardboard signs tucked beneath their rolling luggage, the streets are empty. At sunset, all the buildings in the Capitol sit apollonian in the choleric sunset. The nectarine skies, long since bruised, shrivel to a purple mass of stars. Bars closed, museums shut, and the last calls for trains begin. The night gasps a cool, winter breath as it dies.

The Metro lives.

Bright lights wave by station on station. Concave square recesses line the cylinders like an opera house. Each flutters by until the train stops. Each stop is a tessellation of the next until the fringes of the District. The trains themselves are great leviathan: coming up for air at either end of their line and the District is its teeming ocean. The insides of these beasts are orange and creamy, metallic and plexiglass. A middle-aged flautist steps off. This leaves the two alone.

Claudia keeps her hair up in tootsie roll pops. Every now and then, she looks up from her screen — trying to make sense of which tessellating cylinder the train flies by. She puts her legs up on the orange cream-sicle seat.

A voice announces over the intercom, "Now at, Bethesda. Next stop, Medical Center."

Claudia looks dead-on toward Padriac and he, perhaps, senses this. He removes an earphone and smiles.

"Aye. This is my stop," he says.

"That's so weird. I'm headed to the hospital."

"What? Why?"

"Someone I know is here. I'm not sure if I should go."

"It's out of my way, but... if you'd like someone."

Claudia's fist unclenches at her side.

"You know what? I wouldn't mind. Follow me, then."

Padriac tosses his head side to side and agrees. Perhaps he has a boring life. Perhaps he is a bit daft. Perhaps he has shit else to do a Friday evening.

★★★

Claudia and Padriac walk the long stair to the surface. They emerge from the station under that mass of bruised sky. The steel canopy looks like a clam's shell. Claudia's sweater is starting to unravel around her wrists and her purple beanie holds back her long hair, which is darker than a priest's heart in Catholic School.

"You're strange, Claudia."

"Oh, I'm strange all right, but I'm no stranger. Go

ahead. Ask me anything."

"Why'd you ask me to follow?"

Her eyes shift toward the hospital and back again.

"It's my mother."

"Your mother asks you to invite strange men on subways to walk with you at 2 a.m.?"

"My mother waters petunias on her front porch back in Arizona…"

Claudia goes on about her mother and her biological father, how her mother had run away from home. How her father wore stupid bolo ties and used to step on her mother's toes. How her mother kept petunias in a pot and buried her father's ashes in it one winter in Arizona.

Padric opens his mouth but just bites his lip and turns toward the medical center's towers.

Claudia stops speaking at that, looking off at the Medical Center's floodlights and the Security Gate. Specks of snow get caught in her hair. An ambulance passes.

Padriac breaks the silence: "What does that have to do with this hospital?"

Claudia's eyes trail off like a deer that's crossed a highway.

"My mom eventually married after my father died. That man is a patient here."

"I'm sorry."

"Don't say that. You don't even know him."

★★★

Inside the emergency room doors is a guard with a walkie-talkie and a dark blue sport coat. He flirts with the Navy nurse, who flicks her wrist at him and returns to a row of charts. A janitor mops the floor in quick s-shapes, listening to a tinny boombox. The streaks shine upward.

Claudia drags Padriac by the hand and he tilts his head. The two trundle over white tiles. Perhaps, this is a dream for Padriac, head still shaking, hand half anxious to pinch himself, if only because that's what people are supposed do.

"There he is," she says.

Inside a small hospital room, in a mess of wire and tubes, the man rests supine. His gaunt face stares at the ceiling. The room smells like rubbing alcohol poured into a latrine in June. What few lights remain burn dimmer as she enters—as if each steps gloms their being.

"Stand outside, Padriac."

Claudia enters the room. The door slides closed behind her. She walks a few paces, moving slower and slower as she nears the bed until she stops. Claudia rakes at her frayed sweater sleeve. The lower end comes off, threads dangling like bile dripping in a slaughterhouse. She looks at the emaciated face of the man in the hospital bed. His eyes are open but he doesn't stir as she approaches.

She offers him the scrap of her now torn sweater. Her hand quavers at first. When she sees his hands—those coarse hands like the tendrils of a squid—that her own hands steady. Her breath evens. This is what a stone precipice must feel like all year round.

Claudia stuffs the knitted scrap into the man's mouth and slaps the side of his head. He does not recoil or blink. His face just slacks over, defeated.

"Speak to me," she says.

Silence, he gives.

"Speak."

Drool pools on the pillow, with the glassy eyes, immobile.

Padriac pushes the door aside and grabs Claudia by the waist, her face scalding over as she bites into her own lips. Her impotent hands claw at his arms. The heart monitor beats. No bruises form.

"Speak!"

★★★

The two sit at the Metro Station.

Padriac lifts his gaze as if to query but cuts himself short. Somewhere else, a nurse also wonders why a comatose man feeds on a black sweater.

~49~

Claudia shakes her head as she sees him do this.

"Tell me a story, Padriac. Tell me about you."

"As a boy, I'd visit my cousins in Washington—the State, mind you. Whatcom Falls. Dead of summer, right? Days muggy and thoughts melting together and a hope of a coke from the vending machines at the park's head. We'd jump into wading pools. There were these girls my age—new to two-piece bathing suits—when we weren't, you know, jumping. I had this crush on this fair haired one—Zuzana. I nearly stole her top."

"Lechering bastard," Claudia says. "You must've been pleased with yourself." She starts to notice his eyes drooping. Padriac's brogue turns even the letter 'R' into a soft purr, like a child's boots jumping through puddles too shallow to splash.

"Well—it isn't a trout until it's on the bank, right? The park blew up one day: a gas leak mixed with boys and fireworks. A fishery used to hatch upstream from the wading pools. My cousins woke me that afternoon and told me to look outside. I could see it from the hill their house was on: a coarse, black mushroom cloud to the south.

"It's funny—I saw it ten years later and the place is greener than it ever was."

Padriac and Claudia board the train. Muted lighting

above. The train's grime forms a home. Padriac's eyes nod further. He drifts to sleep at the sound of the tracks humming just below.

★★★

Padriac and Claudia reach the end of the escalator.

The entirety of Dupont Circle is draped in snow. All the sharp angles of the Fountain are rounded by thick tufts of powder. Tracks double back on themselves and it's not clear where one person's path ends and another begins.

A couple watches their young daughter build a snowman, scrapping together branches for the arms and a fallen CCTV camera for one of the eyes.

"Would you look at that? All proper with that monocle."

The dark rings beneath Claudia's eyes fade.

"You know—he just needs…" Claudia starts. She begins tearing at her sleeve. The fibers unwind and it's off soon enough. Claudia folds it together in a bundle. "He needs a scarf."

Claudia walks forward. She hands the black sleeve to the young girl. The girl's parents look on, uncertain. The child smiles wide, like a cartoon character eating a pie in a single bite. She wraps the sleeve around the snowman's neck.

Claudia steps back. The CCTV camera rests dilapidated, looking down on the scarf, like a sad clown. Padriac chortles, like air leaking from a balloon.

"And you say I'm a foreigner." Padriac pauses, stomach rumbling. He motions toward a diner. "Want a bite? I'd've eaten at the hospital but their food—it never sits well."

Standing Room

Upper Division

Eliska attended a liberal arts college in the Pacific Northwest where students held candlelight vigils for the dwindling moose populations in Northern Saskatchewan, despite none of the students having actually seen Saskatchewan, save for a sophomore who only had fond memories of hunting moose on snowmobiles with her now deceased father—but she was Canadian and that's to be expected. They'd cure her of her nostalgia.

"Is that man dressed as a satyr?" Eliska asks, looking outside.

"Sort-of. He's in independent study," Aaren says.

"How independent?"

"Well, he's dressed as a satyr."

The school possessed avant-garde names for courses—things like "Urban Pastoral: Discombobulants in the American Wasteland" or "On Being, Then Nothingness: Why Nihilism Matters" but the course names were tangential at best. The school boasted of its diversity. This really meant it devolved into making many feel like they didn't belong—an ironic subversion of their raison d'être.

The buildings on campus were built offset to one another—like M.C .Escher paintings. Yet walkways never ran perpendicular. They ran at odds. Eliska sits in the building's foyer with her writing group: Aaren, Glen and Laquida. She taps her feet, keeping 6/8 time like a Venetian gondolier's barcarole. Each time Aaren looked up, she buried her eyes in her work. He sits not accidentally across from her. She hopes. They'd been dating a week—so, perhaps, he'd better.

Each collection of writing for class was labeled "blocks." Imagine the first words that come to mind when you associate writing and blocks. Eliska thinks of jumping out windows. Still, none of this changes the fact a half-naked man whinnies on the campus lawn.

★★★

Inside, no one believes the professor's smile.

"What unique insight could you offer us into Nietzsche's line, Glen?"

Glen rolls his eyes and breathes. His cheeks fume at

the calling-to-attention-ness, the Professor assuming he would have a different interpretation, from the onset, of such a simple line. Laquida grimaces. It was the third time this week that a question had been prefaced that way.

"Nietzche's commenting on how Europe acted as if God were dead, regardless of religious belief." Anyone could've answered the question but no one else in the course had questions phrased that way by the professor. Glen doesn't need to be reminded of differences. That's what the real world and families are for. There's a reason Glen doesn't go to temple or tell anyone of his bat mitz-vah.

The professor returns to the board, tossing the chalk to his writing hand. He smiles.

"I fucking hate this school," Glen says, resting his forehead on the desk.

Laquida rests her head down too. A student asked her earlier if she'd seen anyone die in Iraq or Afghanistan while in the Army. Some questions don't need prefac-ing—they need un-asking. So, she faces Glen, both heads on the desk.

"Glen?"

He grunts and turns his head to face her—both rest-ing on their side.

"Count me in."

★★★

"Eliska—I want to tell you something," Aaren says.

The blood leaves Eliska's face. "Tell you something?" So imperial. His apartment is clean, she thinks. Aaren's well-dressed. He doesn't think he's Kurt Cobain. The thoughts boil over like Alka-Seltzer. This is the part where he comes out of the closet. Or says he's married. Or is going to jail. Please, let it be jail. Washington State prisons had conjugal visits. Just my luck. I look like Mrs. Robinson but I draw like Mrs. Hutchinson.

"I like you," Aaren says.

"Oh. Really? That's sweet of you." Don't let him know you like him. The blood flushed back again—she feels it in her chest. Is this what a heart-attack feels like?

"There's a show tonight..."

"I'll go."

★★★

The satyr, Robin Goodfellow, listens to "Night-club-bing." He wonders what dance the atomic bomb is and if his parent's '94 Impala can haul two ice-chests worth of hard cider. He'd spent a quarter finding the perfect yeast: Aphroditus draughtii—which grew on local ferns. Robin hums as he drags the chests.

Class over—the writing group approachs.

"This makes no sense," Robin says.

Laquida grabs one of the chests and helps. "What's the story, Robin?"

"Exactly. Sun's set and there isn't one. A story that is. I'm a cog in the big wheel."

Robin rolls his head on its base, cracking the vertebrae. He hands a bottle of cider to each member of the writing group.

"If there's a point, it's that I hold the microbrews."

★★★

"I'm blocked up," Eliska says. She moves her bookbag to the floorboard.

"You drank Robin's cider?!" Aaren asks.

"No—for class."

"Oh. Armchair critics and their six shooters?"

Eliska nods, turning onto Cooper Point.

"Anyone's an author: not just loners with large bookcases or MFAs who sat bored in Brit Lit," Aaren says.

"Just write?"

"Right. You got a story tell?"

"Not yet," Eliska says. She looks at the gas pedal. "Talking about nothing makes everything better—makes me clear-headed."

"That isn't what they'd put on a Hallmark card," he says. Eliska laughs as Aaren continues: "So, are you—

clear-headed?"

"Only if what you're saying means nothing."

Aaren smirks. "Was it obvious?"

"You had no idea what you were saying, did you?"

"No—not at all."

★★★

Goebbels stands in the dairy isle—not *the* Goebbels but a Goebbels. He stares at rows of mass-produced, organic, soy, and almond milk. Only one was homogenized. It wasn't organic.

"Corporations. What a bunch of—" Goebbels begins. His boots polished a Hello-Kitty black, a swatiska on his arm: he means business. His faux-tribal tattoos scream "don't fuck with me—I come from an upper-middle class suburb."

Robin passes Goebbels as everyone looks on. He runs his fingers through his blonde afro and speaks: "A convenient scape goat."

"What?" Goebbels asks. He walks over to the writing group, eyeing each. Eliska thinks of bonobo pseudo-sexual dominance rituals. Everyone else would think it a "faux-paux."

"Keep walking," Laquida says. "I've never been afraid of a ginger."

Goebbels laughs. His mustache looks like the casting

call from a 70s porno.

"You're all right," Goebbels says. He wipes his hand down his face then knifes his hand toward Glen. "Just take your little shiksa with you."

"Aw, fuck no." Glen breaks from Laquida's hand. "Take your Ziggy Heil-dust with you, ya creep!"

Glen lowers his back leg and extends his shoulder into a perfect blow—the kind that Glen's 105 pounds needs when beating eco-friendly, white supremacists with carnie mustaches. Goebbels drops like butter in a warm skillet.

No one speaks as Robin rests on his haunches and turns Goebbel's head side-to-side.

"Poor bastard didn't realize his role in the narrative."

Glen grabs half-and-half and turns to his writing group. Aaren and Eliska avoid eye contact but Laquida grins They walk in silence to the cash register. The checker bags their goods.

"I'm so sorry. Is that a skin condition?" the checker asks—having seen the fight.

"What is?" Glen asks.

She gestures toward Glen's scalp.

"That's my haircut."

★★★

The moon hangs high as the Perseids scratch the sky's

pavement. Aaren and Eliska walk an abandoned rail line near downtown.

"You want to write? Write me. Tell me the story you've made."

Eliska teeters on the edge, looking off into the mud flats. She holds her arms out. Aaren walks without wobble.

"You mean guess?"

She notices that Aaren doesn't bother sticking his arms out—his feet keep planted.

"You're certain of something. Don't tell me—you know the meaning of life?"

"Life has no inherent meaning," Aaren says.

Eliska stopped on the rail tracks. "Why go on then?"

"Who wants 'nothing killed me' on their epitaph?"

Eliska stands closer to Aaren, leaning against him to steady herself. His breath rolls over her nose like the tide of smooth beach stones. The gap between them closes and—she turns, walking down the line. Eliska looks over shoulder.

"How do you sleep with yourself?" Eliska's stomach gnaws like feral hamsters as she asks this but Aaren'd snuck up on her heart with the subtlety and grace of a ball-pein hammer.

★★★

Olympia's 4th oldest Buzzcocks tribute band plays over stereo. They shake, rather. The blacked-out club downtown smells like apple-cinnamon potpourri, thanks to a surplus of organic incense candles right as the New Age mysticism market fell out in the early 2000s—when venture capitalists were already bleeding from the tech bubble and didn't have enough for the out-of-body bubble.

The writing group stood around the older artist's gallery.

"Art's like the song. It seems so real but you can't touch it." The painter strokes his wisp of a mustache. His black shirt and thick hair make his old, blue eyes sear with the suns of his native Azerbaijan.

"How long does it take?" Laquida gestures to the painted fruit, glistening, with ants crawling over orange peels. The punk group finishes their set.

"Old style? Classical painting—like the Flemish masters. A few months—most drying."

"Do they sell?"

The painter leans back and laughed, his gut shaking like a pack of dogs. His crow's feet to his wrinkles form a mane.

"People want to break the rules before they master them.

"I paint for a living but I fish for the soul—and so I can eat."

★★★

Eliska shifts her feet on the floorboards as each car left—waving good-bye to Glen and Laquida. Aaren slides into the passenger seat. Eliska reaches over him to close the passenger door and she apologizes.

"For what?" Aaren asks.

"For what I said on the tracks."

"Wait—you were being mean?" Aaren laughs. "You need to work on that."

"Do I now?"

Down the road Eliska thinks she sees a deer—but it's Robin. He keeps his hands in his pockets, staring up at the stars. She pulls over.

"Robin, great beer. You need a ride?"

"No. I'm fine—cog in the wheel, remember?" Robin says.

"Are you sure?"

"Of my place in the greater narrative? Yes.

"But I'll be all right," Robin says. "The world's hard but hardly serious."

Eliska nods and then drives off watching Robin in the rearview mirror. He blows into his hands. A deer exits the woods and walks alongside him. Robin look up and laughs in the night, alone, and he fades into the road.

"Must be lonely—lonely knowing everything." She looks over at Aaren who, for all his deconstruction of meaning, smiles. She thinks of all the times Aaren didn't fit her narrative, how Glen rested his head on tables each day and how Flemish masters fished so they could eat. Eliska turns the steering wheel. "Would you like coffee? I can make some at my place?"

Aaren mulls over the words.

"That depends."

"On what?"

"On what you'd like for breakfast."

★★★

Glen hangs his trucker cap next to the picture of his father. He'd been ice fishing at Gull's Lake in Minnesota when his father died. On the first play of the fourth quarter, when Pittsburgh lost their third turnover, the ice gave and down his father went. He was ten. So, he went to live with his mother in Camp Verde, Arizona.

Glen grabs two beers from the fridge door and opens them on his belt buckle. He grew up resenting that. Others thought it made him look like a hick. In truth, it reminds him of his father. His dad.

"What sign are you?" Glen asks.

"I don't believe in bullshit," Laquida says.

Glen frowns. "My dad's an Aquarius. Or was, any-ways."

"I'm sorry, honey."

"Don't be—there's no meaning to it. They're just stars."

"Mustn't it mean something to you?"

Glen tilts the bottle. He sets the beer down on the front porch, leans back and stretches an arm toward the sky.

"I wanted to show you his constellation."

★★★

Eliska looks at her pile of laundry. She used to frown when people saw it but she feels the indentation in bed alongside her. Her room, the coldest in the house, lulls its spell as she pulls the sheets up over her shoulders.

Reaching one leg backward, Eliska feels the back of Aaren's feet with her toes. They are smooth on the heel, unlike hers. He never wore sandals. Moving to the soles, she finds callouses. They don't match her preconceptions and part of her hopes Aaren won't wake.

Upper Division

Killing the Messenger

Minali Soong hears a cartridge scratch vinyl next door. Her neighbor, a young man whose name she forgets, listens to records after work. On some nights, she finds her hips swaying side-to-side. Tonight, she cooks corned beef hash. The only bread left at the corner store earlier was naan which reminds her of her mother. Minali doesn't finish.

Still, she likes the sense of it while listening to her neighbor's records. She loved the smell of warm bread and the way the loaf folds on her tongue.

Her neighbor plays "Break On Through" by the Doors—one of those songs that had the chorus in parentheses. It reminds her of the night she'd lost her virginity. She'd gone out with friends to a Karaoke parlor in Pomona and a cute boy with short and black sat next to her. He asked if she was Cuban. She felt herself recede at the time but didn't want to explain the history of her Chinese father nor her Indian mother—since she neither came from nor saw nor ever had interest in either country. Instead, she let the boy kiss her and sang out of key. The next morning, she gathered her things and left. At home, her mother shouted, asking if she wanted to disgrace the family. Her father didn't speak. He pulled a bottle of whiskey from the top of the fridge and poured two glasses.

That—that was then but here she sits on a Thursday night. She unpacks Alka-Seltzer into a glass. Next door, the record finishes. Seven tracks bleed through the walls. The needle scratches off. As she washes her plate in the sink, her neighbor turns the record over. Minali holds on to herself.

★★★

The neighbor, Bradan Doyle, kicks the sheets. He tries the sheep-counting, toe-flexing and a nightcap. He drank a few earlier—to be safe. The shadows move along the walls as he wonders why he's never seen Gibraltar. Each movement of his toes suffers a delayed response— as if every action queues. Bradan sits and watches. He grows to hate his internal complaints and laundry lists.

Moving into the kitchen, he cooks broccoli chicken before six dumbbell curls. He copies and pastes, rinses and drains, lathers and repeats before heading back to bed. His nights feel warm and strange.

Prior to prison, Bradan possessed little desire for a steady job. He quit his first nine-to-five over its, well, nine-to-fivedness and a gig as a living statue ended in an ornithological accident. He finds it ironic that a conviction now bars him from most employment.

To be a man of few convictions, he thinks, is a great thing indeed. He was lucky to have finished a degree in psychology before serving time.

In prison, Bradan learned to speak when absolutely necessary. A fellow inmate, a big Samoan named Tama, once asked what he'd done. He never could tell if Tama was cut from steel or fat—just that he never wanted to cross him. He didn't answer until Tama leaned forward. That's all Tama did with anyone.

Bradan said he'd built a pig sty on his sister's property in Utah, one for her daughter's FFA project. He didn't have the permits. The maximum sentence was six months.

Tama laughed, his long hair falling from his bandana. He'd come in for marijuana possession.

"You're here because you built a fence?"

He nodded.

"Half the legislators want to put a fence around Mexico but you put a fence around pigs..."

Bradan laughs to the memory as the rain patters down the window.

★★★

Minali sketches a ragged dog on a legal pad at work. The suits from Google talk about the latest cellphone—and how her company fits into their portfolio of mobile patents. There's a joke from a smiling exec who brushes his hair back. He talks about how much social media brings people together and Minali frowns at the prospect of 140 characters redefining "together." She hoped there'd be more artistry in a tweet, like a poet reducing words. At the thought of instant, constant communication, she cringes. Minali wrote letters as a kid—ones that she'd read over and plan. The internet lost that spirit—that weighting of words and making them count. Her ex-fiancé, Ari, and she wrote long ones, each paragraph and break foreplay to the brief weekends they'd spend in Seattle. They sexted once. She wasn't sure how she felt about emoticons.

As the Google executive sips his Chai and discusses branding potential, Minali draws a balding retriever. Shagged, unkempt tufts of hair stick out while others are missing. She does so from memory.

Ari and she used to ski on Mount Baker and one day, they saw a stray dog emerge from the woods. He wagged his tongue and trotted along the riverbed. Neither of them spoke until they reached the lifts.

"I had a dog like that," Ari said. He shifted his googles. They sat on the lift and he put his arm under hers, glove on glove.

At the top, Ari's skis snagged on a fixture. She held his hands and tried to pull him free, all-the-while yelling at the ski lift operator. She pushed her open palm forward. The operator took this as a sign to speed up. There was a crack as Ari's body hit the ledge. When the medics came, Minali still held Ari's hands. His legs and torso rested just feet away.

That past winter, she returned to the slope. She'd put a Star of David up on a painter's stick. Ari never spoke about religion. He never went to temple. However, he kept a Star of David on his keychain. He used to, anyways. "Used to." She hated the simple past tense. On the drive from her makeshift memorial, she saw the stray dog again—running off into the Parks Service trail alongside a heavier, shorter one.

When the meeting concludes at five, Minali clocks out: both at work and on her couch, where she naps.

That's all she gets out of sleep these days.

★★★

Bradan counsels a student at the University of Washington. He covers his yawn. Bradan isn't used to so many people just a few years younger complain about their parents. Prison inmates complain less. Outside, pedestrians walk by his window, hoods drawn. He wonders why so few in Seattle carry umbrellas.

He remembers his first case: Corporal Williams, an Afghanistan veteran from Duluth. Bradan managed Williams' case for the Veterans' Affairs office. He'd done his residency at the National Naval Medical Center in Bethesda.

Williams told his story, a cigarette between his fingers: how he'd been a fresh NCO in a combat zone, driving a HMMWV in a convoy through a city. A local boy waved at his vehicle. He wore the same Teenage Mutant Ninja Turtle shirt Williams wore as a kid. He thought the world a smaller place as he waved back. Next thing he remembered, he was on a stretcher with a corpsman marking his forehead with a sharpie. The Corpsman asked how many fingers he saw. Williams said four.

"He told me I'd be balls deep in Landstuhl. He said 'save a beer.'"

Williams's left thigh shook like a Shetland pony. The

other sat on a steel replacement, just above the knee. Bradan's eyes averted the rubber end-cap on the stub and tried to focus on Williams' own eyes.

"You can ask," Williams said.

A Sergeant finished his cigarette and turned toward Williams, "Would you mind if I paid a hooker to jerk off with your prosthetic?"

Corporal Williams laughed. There was a sense that the tourniquet took only his leg, not his life. He'd been so desperate for someone to mention it that even such a comment put him at home. The phantom limb's pain eased as Williams regained his bearing.

Bradan covers his yawn again. His patient complains about how uncertain he is of his identity and how he wished his parents would pay his cellphone bill. The student calls them "bourgeois." At times, Bradan thinks himself the pedestrian and not the passersby outside.

★★★

Both Minali and Bradan leave their apartments at the same time, the same sharp pang in their chests but neither rougher for the wearing. They enter the elevator with the number three over top. Bradan inhales, deep and sharp, as Minali passes. Neither hits the button.

"Is that garlic?" Bradan asks.

Minali isn't sure she hears him right. Of all the conversations she hoped she'd have with her neighbor, this wasn't on that list.

"I need to stop. It makes my breath smell bad."

She goes to reach for the button but Bradan beats her there. He hits the ground floor.

"I like garlic," Bradan says.

★★★

The two enter separately but, on a Friday night, they might as well enter together. The smell of burnt grinds chokes out the café. The ropes for the queue wind back and forth. He thinks that it's as if the whole world stood waiting for their time, their number to be called. Until then, everyone waits. Minali queues beside him.

"Bradan, right?"

He nods. Standing in line, he can't decide whether Pumpkin Dulce de Leche is the best or worst idea ever. "Here for coffee?" he asks.

"It's a hot spot," Minali says. The barista offers the dessert, foaming spilling over into the grating.

Bradan waves good-bye. He reaches into his pocket for the order number but it's slipped through. A thought flashes through his head, the absurd kind one finds at night that wonders whether his number will be called, if no one is there to answer.

★★★

"Where do you live again?" the screen flashes. Bradana told this anonymous stranger once that he worked on the exchange floor—which he didn't. He'd said that. He also spelled color without a "u." That left Chicago and New York.

Bradan looks out over the U District: fluorescent street lamps in ne'er-ending rain, the streets with more coffee stands than people walking on them and the pale fire of the Space Needle. The radio towers on Queen Anne Hill flicker to an unseen rhythm section. The rains—those rains that drive more suicides per year than Palestine.

"Manhattan," he types. He nods his head as he looks up at the fountain. Lights line the bottom of it. Plumes of water swell up from the ground like a down feather in a hurricane.

"What are you looking for in a person?" Bradan hesitates. He can't write the truth: that'd he'd want someone warm next to him. That's too basic, too elemental. So, he lists traits at odds: no-nonsense but polite, educated but fun-loving, nice face but not superficial. The list grows into everything without saying anything. He won't say that he wants someone to clean his fingernails for. He tries not to admit that he'd settle for anything. Honesty, he felt, seemed to alienate the polite. It takes a crude and vulgar mind to accept the entirety of a person. The same mouth he might kiss could curse too; it could recede into a vowel or curl in a consonant.

"Would you go for someone like me?" the screen asks. Bradan's keystrokes agree.

Across the way, Minali also writes. Her heart flutters a bit and cheeks warm at the prospects on her screen. She flirts with a man from Manhattan. The man seems, though distant, writes like a warm coat. She wishes they could meet. "The sun is rising in London," she writes. They flirt back and forth, so self-aware to never tell the truth; so unaware that their messages travel greater distances to reach each other than they would if they stood and said hello.

Both wish each other a good night and promise to meet someday. When standing, Bradan and Minali repeat the exchange, without the same thoughts. Neither realizes who their anonymous lovers are. Minali holds a grin on her face as she looks up at Bradan. He's deep in thought over this mystery woman in London.

The final call of the night is made on the ticket queue: the number one.

The two exit together. Minali laughs as Bradan strolls alongside her.

"Have a good night?" he asks.

"I did. I met someone on the internet."

Minali slides her arm over his. They lock at the elbow. As she does this, Bradan looks up. He feels a wedge loosen near his heart. Minali see it in his face and drags him into skipping along Aurora Avenue. Minali can't remember the last time she did this. They stop at Seattle Center, walking up to the fountain. Lights line the bottom of it. Plumes of water swell up from the ground like a down feather in a hurricane. The fountain's bursts are synchronized to Mozart's Requiem Mass. He wrote it before he died.

Mist forms and the structure bursts a white jet into the air.

Minali now begins to regret the same fiction that Bradan tells. Neither speaks though—the night crisper than an apple and the taste it too sweet for either to trespass each other's ground. So, they sit and watch the water return to the ground. It's a lost fight against gravity.

★★★

Bradana wishes Minali a good night when they return to their apartment complex.

"Good luck with your boyfriend in New York," he says. "Let me know how it turns out."

Minali thanks him and they wave goodbye. Inside, she throws her purse on the couch and unwraps her scarf. She lets it slide off her nape. There was a sense in her blood that life is like a brilliant punch-line whose only fault is timing. In that heart-beat, through the wall, Bradan's record starts. Minali lies in bed. She removes her glasses and kicks the shoes from her feet, burying them in the blankets.

The record doesn't turn over that night.

Killing the Messenger

d.a. peters

A Human Condition

The first child to die at Ogygia did so of her own volition. That's what other children say.

She'd been picking lotus flowers near the arboretum. The North Sea's rains blew the gutters off the island's sole building. Then the chimney. Then the storm shutters flew off their hinges. A sharp thhpp and off they went across the garden. The girl carried the flowers inside her shawl when the shutter struck. She didn't cry. The wind knocked her to her face and blood foamed from beneath her throat.

A boy next to me said it was her punishment for leaving without the Provosts' permission—and punishment for kissing Stepan on the mouth. He swore he'd seen it. I balled my fist. "Hold your tongue," I said. He said that kissing caused her death. I struck him.

I couldn't see whose face it was through the fogged picture window.

Once the storm subsided, I saw Provot Bláán. The clouds grew darker when he left the building, as if the sun thought to run again. He fastened his collar. He looked around the arboretum, which held spare supplies, and he ran his fingers across the stacks of erasers, blank slates and the bottles of bleach.

Provot Bláán moved the body to the front lawn. He laid her in the grass and tucked his chin in, brow furrowed at the sight. He drew his handkerchief and covered the girl's face. He looked up to the building with its gutters stripped, chimney gone and shutters striking young girls down with flowers in their arms.

In a way, it was like any other orphanage.

★★★

"Polly Jean," Provost MacKay says. "Her name was Polly Jean." He cannot swallow but dares not spit beneath the poplar trees. His black robes gather with a red belt. MacKay is a cordial man: whether the cherries he keeps by his desk or his demeanor with the students. Young and aloof, he often interrupted studies of the Gospels for a joke or anecdote. He was rarely the hero of his stories, something that engendered him to all of us students.

The physician, who sailed five days from Brighton, folds his stethoscope as he sees the gash.

"She was found clothed?"

Provost MacKay nods then leans over, "You don't think she was—"

The physician swats a fly.

★★★

"They aren't coming, Blake" a girl behind me whispers. "Liked her, yes?"

I start to turn but she cuts me short.

"Don't."

All of us, all the sixteen year olds, sit in the basement classroom, waiting for the Provosts to gather us for the funeral. Polly Jean's body's long since gone. In other circumstances, Polly Jean would be an adult but not here, not at Ogygia. The Provosts say the flesh is childish.

There's a tap on my shoulder.

Odessa sits behind me. She whispers about why Provost Bláán kept such an eye on Polly Jean. She says that I'll need to see the library. Her last remark is over the pills they give us each week, the white ones that taste like chalk.

"Don't swallow," she says.

★★★

We line up for our daily bread. I take the cup with

my name marked on it: the blood, the body and the mis-shapen pills of the Lamb.

Provost Bláán begins his sermon, gripping the rod of the cross till his knuckles show:

"In Matthew 23:37, we read of Jesus admonishing Jerusalem for not listening. They killed his prophets and, like a hen who would gather her chicks, Jesus is forced to leave the unwilling behind—leave them desolate.

"My children, you are the eldest at Ogygia and you are here for good—for God. We are your brothers and sisters—so why would students wish to leave us? Is it your fallen condition?"

Some of the children nod. Most of them look up expressionless, as if epitomizing a tabula rasa.

"Then cure yourself of your condition—take the white pill and rest it beneath your tongue. Remove the flesh from your mind."

The other children chew over the sermon. Fast Sunday: the day without food until supper. Despite the nature of this their daily bread, it sat better than a hollow pit.

"The serpents are not yet cast from this garden—this isle of ours. When faced with this, there are two choices: either you give your life to the Lord or you will be cast from the garden. God is a loving God—do not test Him.

Or you will pay as Polly Jean paid."

Provost Bláán asks the children to line up in columns. He dips two fingers into juices made from Orchids and Poppies, swirling them and lapping them up until they pool at the tips—perfection and death, purity and sleep. Three drops drip on each of our heads.

Once released, I wipe the taste from my mouth in a wash basin.

★★★

The redcedar chest opens itself, once I realize how the oblong latch works. The mechanisms overlapped and folded back, yet, it held no lock. I rest my hand on the heartwood, unsure if I should open the container.

The floor creaks and I turn.

"That was hers," Odessa says. She leans against the large bookcase.

"I didn't realize-"

"She didn't want the Provosts seeing it."

"Did they?"

"I think once—but she pushed Provost Bláán away. The birch switch stings; Polly Jean would come in bleeding some nights."

"So, I shouldn't open it?"

"You're not a Provost." She cleans a steadfast knife and stores it in her pocket, pulling her hair back as she approaches.

The weight of the lid grows in my arms.

I feel as though a barbarian in the night appraising the chest's contents: books of varying sizes, the small ledgers they let us write with, sticks of charcoal and rolled paper and a locket box. The first one has sketches over words: blacking out text till a story emerges. What was once medical text had figure nudes now; their mechanical organs replaced with charcoal flesh and fanned veins forming silk. She's taken the bodies the provosts condemned: ephemeral organs with divine purposes and made them into breathing, aching entities. They spill off the pages' margins. Of this, nothing is written in the gutters. Flowers are pressed into the pages: lotuses dissolved into the curves of the figures. Polly Jean wrote—wrote everything. How her stomach would ache pressed against the tables in the mess hall, how the crosses seemed too sensual with the lean, muscular Lord and how her knees would shift when she spoke to certain boys in the school.

Then there's the night Provost Bláán found Polly Jean's collection. The drawings stop for several pages. The figure nude's eyes are sewn shut and a red-black ink forms a hammer. This is no ink like this on the island. The origin hits me like a tethered-ball to the face. I grind my teeth and my shoulders tighten. I smell citrus—something I haven't smelled since Christmas. Odessa places a hand on my arm.

"She never put poppies in the books. They'd fade the drawings and she'd say, 'I'd rather the drawings bleed with me.'"

★★★

The night after Polly Jean died, I lay in bed. Lights out at half past eight. I think of Polly Jean who sang and danced but kept to her books with the flowers pressed in them. Polly Jean who hit harder than the other girls—and knew how to land a punch with her back leg lowered and shoulder extended. Polly Jean who tore the buttons from my blazer in a game of tag because she wanted me to slow down. Polly Jean who kissed one of the other boys—and whose lips "tasted of six pence" or so they said. Polly Jean, the one who knew what she wanted and what lie beyond the island.

So, I pull the blankets closer and masturbate. I think of Polly Jean as the wind howls outside. When done, I feel my shoulders sink, think of this, our daily bread, and cry.

★★★

Provost MacKay teaches the class about the animal kingdom. He musters what enthusiasm he can for the material. The other children said he used to be a professor before he joined his order, that he'd been married and even had child in Brighton. MacKay, in his doubts, makes me wish to believe. He deprecates himself in anecdotes before class: how failed his first exams as a Provost, how he bumbled his way through London. He turns us toward our studies.

On a high table in the back of the room sits a chimpanzee in a large cage. We write how God created all the varieties of animals. The chimpanzee plays on a swing and coos to himself. He braids cloth scraps together into a necklace and admires himself a mirror. He smiles in the cage and folds his arms behind his back, watching.

Odessa passes a note when MacKay's back is turned, drawing her chestnut hair over her right shoulder. I unfold it, pressing it flush against the pages of the schoolbook:

Blake,

A Provost carries a sleeping man on a stretcher. The man comes to and tries to sit straight but his arms are fastened to a board.
"Where am I going?" the man asks.
"You're going nowhere."
"Well, where are you going then?"
"The cemetery."

"The cemetery? But I'm not dead!"

"Well, we're not at the cemetery yet," the Provost says.

Odessa.

P.S. The chimpanzee wonders why we have to study the bible. He knows which side of the glass he's on—and all the more glad.

I finish reading the note and look up. Her eyes twist a smile. The chimpanzee joins in our hoarse laughs.

★★★

"You daft, yeah?" Stepan hits me with a ball. "Don't want to play, do you?"

"Not today."

"You too good for us? Peat sod with two shoes and no soles."

I keep walking across the yard. Past the rows of urns by the fountain, pass the hedgerows that might someday bustle,

I sit on the benches toward the edge of the front lawn, where you can see the white cliffs below and the twin piers jutting from the shore into the wave. I take off my shoes so that only socks remain—knee-high ones whose shape long since gave. The grass brushes against my ankles.

A shadow casts to my side. Two small hands balance a figure behind me—Odessa.

"Polly Jean always liked a game of tag," she says.

Odessa kneels down, resting a shawl of flowers before her and a bowl, lowt and lotus. She wrings the swollen flowers through her hands causing a violet fluid to fill the vessel.

"You can help, if you'd like. These are for paints."

I leave my shoes and sit next to Odessa. She passes a cluster of the flowers to me and I hold them with both hands full. Interlocking my fingers, I rub back and forth, until the drops fall.

Odessa leans over and begins to whisper about the time Polly Jean and her pinned a note to the Provosts robes and how they'd talk long into the night and wondered if anyone else on the island, or the waters round it, or if the world felt the same. Her breath is warm in the early spring. The spring storms shake the fence leading to the beach but the wisps of her words fall into my ears like new milk.

★★★

After recess, I visit the Office of Our Father. Provost MacKay sits there, head held in hand, as he writes. I knock on the door and he motions for me to come forward. He puts his pen back in its fountain.

"If it isn't Blake? Please, sit." He gestures to the chair before him, the one with red lacquer, motifs of snakes eating their tails, and snow swirling around them. "Playgrounds can be rough. I remember your age."

My eyes fall to the floor. It's an adult speaking to a child—not a human to another human.

"You didn't have a problem with lunch, did—"

"Is there a God, Provost?"

Provost MacKay leans back in his chair. His hands rub the leather arm rests back and forth. "I hope so."

I explain Polly Jean's journals: how the figures had their eyes struck out from them when Bláán took Polly under his care, the dandelion nooses and what Odessa told me. I say that there's a reason she was found in her state that day.

"You've said too much."

I don't hear a noise after he speaks, not a creak nor a footstep. Provost Bláán's cold hand rests on my shoulder.

★★★

Streaks of blood line the floor as I wake.

Standing, my legs give way at the knee. The once brick blood grows black and flakes. There's a bone-deep pain from the bruises and a popping sound. I don't know what it is.

I will not die at Ogygia.

Odessa grabs me by my waist and throws my arm over her shoulder. She tells me the supplies are late form the mainland, so the Provosts will cancel tomorrow's classes.

"They keep all the wood for their hearth."

She carries past the boys' domicile.

"Aren't I—"

Odessa faces me and shakes her head back and forth against my own. She carries me up the stone staircase. Bounds books line the same shelves from this past month. She lays me on wool sheets. I'm shivering and she crawls into the blankets behind me. The front of her dress must be covered in blood but she holds me there.

"I'll stay—just fall asleep."

★★★

The second child to die did so at Ogygia. Whether it was her own volition doesn't matter—not now, not for all the years under sun.

Word spread that Odessa, the girl with sharper heart than sharper eyes, stuck Provost Bláán through with a steadfast knife. One, two, one, two: back, throat, then jowls. One for Polly, one for me, and for her completely. The Provost fell as fast he stepped. So, that's the Holy trinity—so that's the wandering scythe beneath which worms will writhe. No liturgies or effigies or sodomies— just black cloak on the floor and the fallen, the departed.

Church bells beat not as choirs of angels but drums of dogs—lead laden ones that shake the earth. Everyone is gathering to see what seeds a man wrought.

Such are his wages.

Odessa carries my weight down to the pier. The other children are either asleep or helping the Provosts. We fall into a boat. There are maps, a compass made from wood and tins of food.

"I'll return," she says. Blood still soaks her shirt but for all its grotesqueness the patterns pool and form into those fanned veins that Polly Jean drew. Odessa runs up the cliff trail—and I see her goal: Polly's chest—that seemed to birth escape.

I am not the only one to notice. Stepan stands at the trail's head. He sees Odessa then turns toward me. Blood soaks her shirt. Odessa grips the side latches and runs with the chest.

Stepan's running toward the warning bell and, in through the blood caked on my eyes, I see a figure grab his arm. Provost MacKay stands there, his red cheeks a new shade of pale in the afternoon sun. Stepan protests, says that no one is allowed to leave. The Provost watches Odessa untie us. She pushes with her legs and the tide drags the boat away until that island is a rock on the horizon.

★★★

With my face against the glass, I can no longer see the other ships as they leave. The island itself is gone—so far gone that there's water, sky and the slow, slant horizon line between. The further I go into the horizon, the more I realize that the sky and sea do not touch. You'd think they'd meet but you could travel the whole way round the world and only wind up where you began: with a sky and a sea and nothing between—nothing except Odessa and I.

"What'll we do now?" Odessa asks. "Where will we go?"

I think over her words as the blanket covers us and the red sunset frackles through the porthole.

"That's just it: we'll go; we'll make do."

The air heaves from my throat and my eyes burn. I laugh because my wish comes true: the third child to die did not do so at Ogygia.

A Human Condition

d.a. peters

Curious Branding

The painting hangs straight in the hospital—the only one like it. There's a shepherd, a ploughman and a ship. They're busy. A body rests in in the water behind them—rests with rumpled feathers. None of them notice a leg sticking out.

My daughter, Judith, colors. She looks at the painting from time to time, holding her crayons up in the air. She squints then settles on "canary." The doctor hands her another piece of scratch paper from a legal pad before smiling at me.

"Do you like to swim?" the doctor asks.

Judith nods her head. "I'm a good swim-mer."

It's cold between my legs and the instrument she uses can only be a cheese grater. When she finishes, I gather the hospital gown and sit up. My right breast falls like a rubber band. The doctor says I'm lucky that they caught it early, if it's what she thinks it is. Her fingers are covered in ink from my chart. I ask her what the odds are. She says the mortality rate's low.

"About the same as Queen High," she says. "Like lowball poker."

"I don't play."

She closes her mouth. Her eyebrows sink but she forces a laugh. "We'll know more once the biopsy comes back."

"How much?"

She looks at the charts and pulls out the x-ray. "The incision shouldn't be larger than a quarter."

"Cost—I meant cost."

She smiles and tells me not to worry. "Insurance will cover it."

I nod and tell her I don't have any. The doctor frowns this time. I inhale: crisp and sharp.

"I'm sure something can be worked out." She hand me the forms and adds, "You're all set." She draws the curtain as she leaves.

I start to dress. "Baby, start putting your crayons in the box."

Judith puts them in one-by-one. She rolls the paper

into a tube and stores it in the empty space in the carton.

"Were the doctor's hands cold?"

"Yeah, baby, they were cold."

★★★

My upstairs neighbors test the suspension on their mattress once a month—either that or they jump on the bed. They could pull the headboard from the wall. One lamp fall from calling my landlord, I see the glow of my answering machine. Two messages wait for me.

"Hello? Vera?" the first asks. "This is Ravi. I'm getting married." The machine finishes with his number. I didn't realize he had a phone.

Ravi and I once rode for a month on motorcycles. He bought fruit from road stands. I peeled them. We wound up lost in a cemetery in New Orleans. I told a skeeving camera crew to insert their Mardi Gras beads into their "orifices with particular force." They looked stunned. Ravi shot beer through his nose and laughed. Once, when money ran dry, Ravi fought an Army Sergeant in a match outside Topeka. The Sergeant called him a "haji towelhead." Ravi won in the first round with a knock-out.

He didn't speak much until we hit Nebraska but, instead, rested his head on my shoulder at a drive-in. My heart skipped beat like the pulsing radio towers in the distance. That morning, he bought a small, velvet box from a young widow in a flea market.

The second message is from my doctor. The biopsy came back.

★★★

When I call Ravi the following Thursday, a woman named Angel answers the phone. My first instinct is to hang up.

"Is Ravi there?" I don't say another word.

"I'm sorry—he must've stepped out. Can I take a message?"

I expect it. All's right as a morning in May. "I'll call some other time."

I lie back in bed and listen to the crickets outside. Judith kicks the wall in her sleep sometimes. Sometimes it keeps me up but tonight it's comfortable white noise. I think of what I should say, should Ravi call back.

Ravi and I crashed in a cornfield one night in Bum-fuck, Nebraska. We were so far from civilization that I could see the arms of the Milky Way—its thick bands of blue wrapping around white flecks. I couldn't recognize the constellations. All the lights flickered. They cast a plausive penumbra which shone down and, for the first time in my life, I didn't want. Have you ever felt so content that you forget that you ever wanted—anything?

"My father used to say, 'When in doubt, fold,'" I said.

Ravi kicked his boots off near the motorcycles. "Didn't he wind up in Chino?"

I laughed and said it wasn't nice to say but the night's so warm that he only breaks out the military surplus blanket—the green, wool kind. Ravi curled up beside me. His sweat smelled thick and sweet like maple sap. He asked if I wanted to get married. I turned over, looking back at his matted, black hair and his idiot grin forming an open parenthesis.

"If you're still single by thirty-five, yes."

"No, I mean. . ." He looked at the jacket by his feet. With his right root, he pulled it free with his toes. "I mean, will you?"

I held the velvet box—the one from widow in the market. A gold ring sat inside. A pearl pushed against a diamond. "Ravi, I'm not your type."

★★★

I call to my parents. They live in Hurricane—across the state line. My father answers but says that I'd better "talk to your mother." He grunts and walks with the phone.

My mom answers and asks when she's going to see her grandbaby next.

I say I have bad news but her voice shifts like cards

shuffling.

"Not into drugs again?"

So, I inhale and grit my teeth. I tell her about the bi-opsy—how the quarter incision now includes my cervix. I repeat Judith's message to "tell Grandma I love her" and how much Judith misses her and ask whether we can visit once the weekend is over. She says she'd have to ask my father. She goes to hand him the phone but I hear his hoarse breath on the line. He says he's been listening the whole time. He starts choking up.

"I'm here, baby. The line's open."

★★★

When I call Ravi, he answers. His voice is older. He's less jittered than years ago—like ale in an oak cask.

"How are you, Ms. Mischief?"

I tell him that I'm fine—that all is well. He says he's glad to hear that but he's always read me like a traffic light.

"Are you happy, Ravi?"

"It's my wedding. Of course."

I ask when and where.

"Next Sunday. That's the trip: we're getting married in Vegas."

I groan. He gives me the address and says he's going out that weekend for his bachelor party.

"I'll go—but you'd best do right by her."

During my freshman year of college, a boy from my hometown wrote "I love you" in the snow outside my window. Craig Jerome dragged his half-gone shoe on its side, leaving uneven strokes that a crooked brush might— if the canvas were crabgrass. Girls on my floor thought he wrote to them. He ignored them—he ignored everyone: the fraternity coming back from the hockey match with dates in tow, the stray campus unicyclist who regretted his choice of transit.

That night, Craig called from the downstairs lobby. He hoped I felt better.

"Look outside," he said.

When I saw the message, my heart swelled like a balloon—until the congregate fraternity urinated in the snow. Craig looked defeated at the fraternity guys. Ravi was one of them but he helped Craig fix it, piss and all, even patted Craig on the back. That's when I knew I'd get to know Ravi.

★★★

The lights look like a forest fire over the plateau as I drive to work in North Las Vegas. The medication makes me feel like I'm perpetually punched in the gut. I really need a cigarette. I'd like a Saturday night off too but the medication burning a hole in my gut isn't free. In the parking lot, a woman takes off her glasses off. She waves at me.

"You're Karen's daughter, aren't you?"

I nod but I still don't recognize her.

"God, it must've been last year. Your mother asked me to bring a quiche." She pauses . Her hand now rests on my shoulder as she smiles. "You look great—you've lost weight since I last saw you."

"I've got cancer."

Her mouth opens and I think she's done talking for the evening. She leaves, clutching her purse tighter.

As I enter the pub, a man claps his wrists together after read a verse from a small, green bible. The Gideons stamped it.

"Praise Jesus," he says.

Life's a beer. Some hope for the big dramatic whiskey which tastes of earth; others dream of syrup like Schnapps, as if vanilla and butter-rum would fall from a crack in the sky but. . .

Life's beer: staple and filler. It tastes like piss when it first hits—and it's boring. You lose track of the expanses spent drinking the stuff. The buzz comes. You don't even realize how much time you've spent drinking until you've acquired a taste for it, then it's not so bad and you drink enough to forget. You forget how beer tasted when it first hit your tongue.

When I start my shift that night, I drink.

The garish décor makes me wonder how much the lighting bills are. Blacklights are more expensive than brighter, whiter ones. I think about whether I ever really needed to tan. The smoke in these clubs eats skin.

The noise is getting louder in the back and it's irritating the man's bible study. The server's gone out for a break—something about her boyfriend cheating on her. So, I go to the tables in the back, to try and settle them down.

"Can I get you boys anything?"

"Vera!?"

Ravi sits at the head of the table. His friends gather around: a few of them I'd met in passing over the years. He walks around from the table. From the way he turns his head, it's clear he's had too much. He hugs me.

"Vera, I've missed you. Sit with us."

I take a chair and we talk. He's doing well for himself—met Angel at a dealership where he works now. He says he misses the road. I tell him about my daughter, Judith.

"You had a kid? Congratulations." He leans over to hug me again but kisses me on the cheek. I slap him. The table gets quiet at that point.

"Come on--it's my bachelor party. Like old times? "

"Old times were never like this."

He looks down at his beer. "I thought—thought when you asked if I was happy. . ."

I want to tell him everything: why I want him to just be happy. "I need to quit—this, Ravi."

He tips the bottle back and I hope he finds the bottom before I do.

★★★

When I leave the bar, after the last call, I find myself pacing with a cigarette by the stop sign. I swing around it. I used to play with these as a kid—even drove me into physics in college. This is the axis, the fulcrum and I revolve around its center. When I stop, I imagine that the whole world wobbles around the pole and that I am not the one in motion. Give me a place to stand on, and I will move the Earth.

I stop spinning and think about Ravi. There's a rolling boil in my stomach. I want to cough it up. I settle for putting one hand through the plexiglas of a bustop window while the other covers my stomach.

"I'm tired of this self-pity crap."

★★★

Sunday comes and the bridesmaids hold roman candles. Everyone is drunk on pear cider. I sit with my daughter. I recognize only one other guest. I can see why Angel didn't wear a bigger dress as the roman candles start going off into the night sky. The officiator, Mikhail, a big guy who'd been riding for decades, presents them with a clear, green bowl. He blows glass for a living. Ravi and I met him one summer on Montara State Beach. He kept his hair shorter then.

Mikhail says to put their hands inside the bowl. Ravi looks at Angel and raises his eyebrows. She laughs and puts her hand in too. He murmurs about the sun, the moon and the stars. Ravi pulls a box from his back pocket—the same velvet box with the misshapen pearl from a widow in Nebraska. Angel gasps. She throws an arm around him. Ravi and Angel exchange vows.

He's never been fond of religion but loved the shape of it. Mikhail says his piece. They're married now and Ravi carries her to a black Model-T. They're driving back to Los Angeles. He sets her inside before turning around and waving to his friends. He doesn't look my way. Ravi looks happy—he is happy.

So, I exhale.

d.a. peters

Acknowledgements

None of these stories would be here without the careful eyes of the following people (in alphabetical order):

Eddy Brown
August Del Giorgio
Kate Graves
Benjamin Haddix
Steven Hendricks
Will Hoffman
Spike Jordan
Nick Moffitt
Nancy Parkes
Jennifer Peters
Jessica Salas
Julie Schroeder
Sara Shank
Trevor Van Dyke

Each played a role, whether for one or several of the stories. They called me out on my frippery, bullshit and pretention when I needed it. For that, I'm grateful.

d.a. peters

About the Author

D.A. Peters is an author and game designer, most notably *Under the Sink: [Selected Works]*, a collection of short fiction, poetry and photography. A veteran of the United States Marine Corps, he hopes to graduate from The Evergreen State College in Olympia, WA.

d.a. peters